W9-AMS-880

Little Sibu

An Orangutan Tale

For Lorraine Ristic,
with many thanks
—S. G.

Also by Sally Grindley and John Butler:
POLAR STAR

We would like to thank the Orangutan Foundation
for their help in the research for this book.

Published by
PEACHTREE PUBLISHERS, LTD.
494 Armour Circle NE
Atlanta, Georgia 30324
www.peachtree-online.com

This title was originally published as LITTLE TANG in England by Orchard Books in 1998.

Manufactured in Singapore
10 9 8 7 6 5 4 3 2 1
First Edition

ISBN 1-56145-196-7

The Cataloging-in-Publication Data for this title may be obtained from the Library of Congress.

Little Sibu

An Orangutan Tale

Sally Grindley

Illustrated by
John Butler

PEACHTREE
ATLANTA

High up in the treetops of the tropical rainforest, Little Sibu held on tightly to his mother. Hati was devoted to her bright-eyed bundle of orange fur. She fed him and nursed him, kept him clean, and carried him everywhere. At night, she built a nest and curled herself around him. Little Sibu felt warm and safe.

By the time he was three years old, Little Sibu loved to scamper wildly along branches and swing through the trees, but he often asked Hati to carry him. He could feed himself and played at making nests, but he still suckled his mother and took food from her mouth. Hati was always there, ready to give Little Sibu what he wanted.

But now Little Sibu was seven years old. Hati knew he was old enough to learn to look after himself. Soon he would have to live on his own, like other male orangutans, and Hati needed to show him how.

One day, Little Sibu wanted to snuggle up to his mother, but she wouldn't let him. Little Sibu didn't understand. He hung from a branch, squealing angrily and kicking his legs in the air.

Hati moved to a tree close by to nurse Baka, Little Sibu's baby sister. When Hati picked some fruit and put it in her mouth, Little Sibu rushed over and demanded his share. Hati wouldn't give him any. She knew it was important for him to learn to find food for himself.

But Little Sibu didn't want to. He put his hands around Hati's cheeks and tried to open her mouth. She hooted crossly and moved to a higher branch.

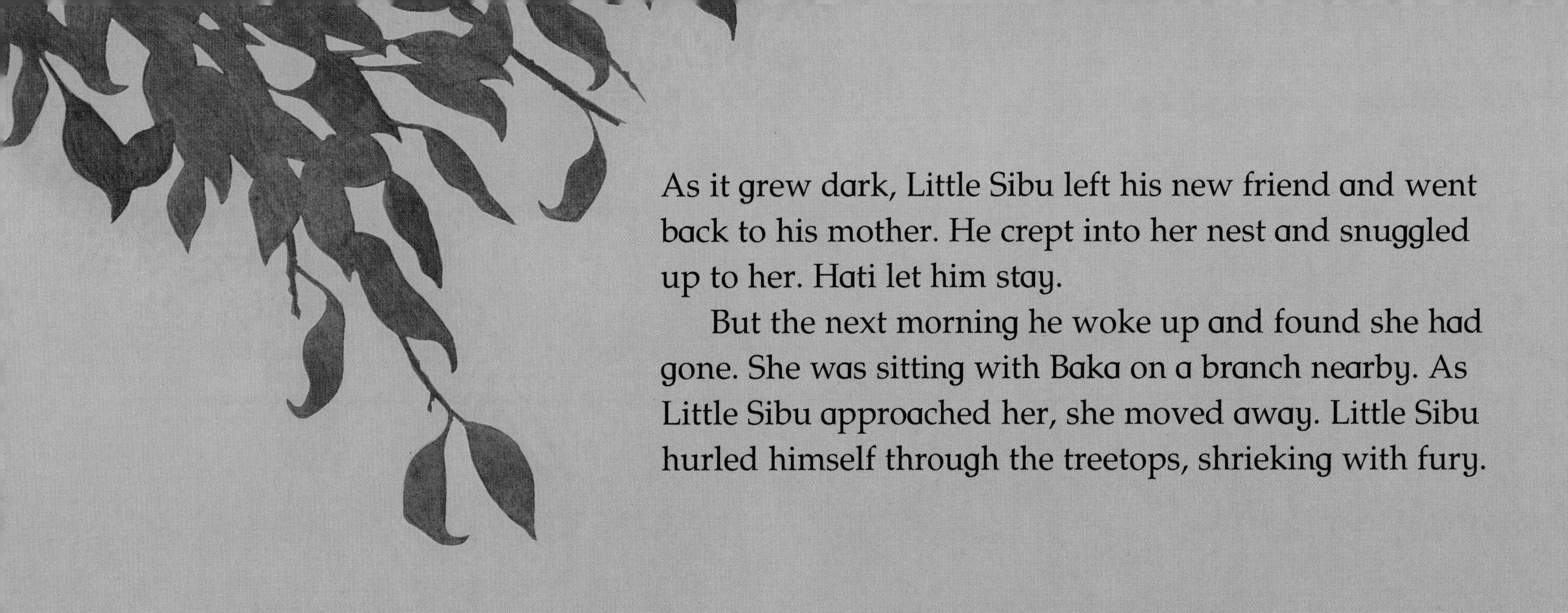

As it grew dark, Little Sibu left his new friend and went back to his mother. He crept into her nest and snuggled up to her. Hati let him stay.

But the next morning he woke up and found she had gone. She was sitting with Baka on a branch nearby. As Little Sibu approached her, she moved away. Little Sibu hurled himself through the treetops, shrieking with fury.

Day after day the same thing happened. Hati wanted to be kind, but sometimes she had to be cruel. She allowed Little Sibu into her nest for a while; then she moved out. She let him play-fight with Baka; then she rushed away with Baka and left Little Sibu on his own. She wanted him to go exploring without her. He always threw a tantrum, but little by little he started to enjoy going off by himself.

Soon Little Sibu began to leave his mother for longer periods of time. He traveled farther away to search for his favorite fruits. He learned to build his own day nests and dozed peacefully. But when night fell, he still went back to Hati and slept in her nest.

One morning, Little Sibu woke to see Hati sucking happily on a durian fruit. Little Sibu loved durian fruit and squealed at his mother to give him some. Then he tried to snatch it, and it dropped to the forest floor. Hati hooted furiously. Little Sibu ignored her and peered down through the branches.

Then he did something he had never done before. He launched himself down through the trees and jumped onto the ground. He began to search frantically for the durian fruit.

Suddenly Hati squealed loudly, but Little Sibu was too busy to notice her warning. Behind him, a tiger crept slowly forward. Hati screamed again. Little Sibu found the durian fruit and leaped up into the trees, just as the tiger pounced and scratched his leg.

Little Sibu squealed with pain and ran to Hati for comfort. She kissed his wound clean and fed him fruit. Later, when it began to rain, she broke off a large leaf and held it over him to keep him dry. Little Sibu enjoyed being mothered again and whimpered quietly as he nestled up to her.

But that night, for the first time, Little Sibu built his own nest. Hati settled down close by, still watching over him.

Little Sibu was sleeping soundly the next morning when Hati went off for the day with Baka. When he awoke, Little Sibu found some food and met up with another young male. They romped and wrestled for a while, then set off through the treetops to find new fruit trees to raid.

As days passed, Little Sibu still spent time with his mother, but more and more often he went off with his playmates or traveled on his own. He found his own food and he built his own nests. Now Hati knew she had done her job well. Little Sibu was happily making his way into the grown-up world.

Orangutan Facts

Orangutans live only in the rainforests of Borneo and Sumatra in Indonesia. In Indonesian, orangutan means "person of the forest." The names of the orangutans in this story are also Indonesian: Sibu (pronounced SEE-boo) means "busy," Hati (HAH-tee) means "heart" or "careful," and Baka (BAH-kah) means "eternal." You might find some orangutans at your local zoo that also have Indonesian names.

Female orangutans are among the most caring, gentle mothers in the animal world. The males do not play any part in rearing their offspring.

A young orangutan will feed from its mother until it is about three and a half years old, and may stay with her until it is about eight. During this time it will learn all the skills needed to survive in the jungle, like how and when to find the best food, how to build a nest, and about parenthood.

Orangutans rarely go to the forest floor, where they may be in danger from tigers and wild boars. They spend their days high up in the trees, where they feed mostly on wild fruit. During the day, they build several different nests from branches and leaves, where they nap. Each night they build another nest.

Orangutans are endangered because large areas of the rainforest have been destroyed, leaving them with fewer and fewer sources of food.

For more information about orangutans, you can contact the

Orangutan Foundation International
822 South Wellesley Avenue
Los Angeles, CA 90049

1-800-ORANGUTAN
www.orangutan.org